BLACK FOREST

A novel by Valérie Mréjen

Translated from the French
by Katie Shireen Assef

Deep Vellum Publishing
3000 Commerce St., Dallas, Texas 75226
deepvellum.org · @deepvellum
Deep Vellum Publishing is a 501c3 nonprofit literary arts
organization founded in 2013 with the mission to bring
the world into conversation through literature.

Published in collaboration with Phoneme Media

PHONEME
MEDIA
www.phonememedia.org

Copyright © 2012 Valérie Mréjen
Translation Copyright © 2019 Katie Shireen Assef

Originally published in French by Editions P.O.L. as *Forêt noire* in 2012

ISBN: 978-1-944700-90-4   ebook ISBN: 978-1-64605-021-5

Library of Congress Control Number: Forthcoming

This book is distributed by Consortium Book Sales & Distribution

Printed in the United States of America

Cover art by Lucas Rollin
Typesetting and graphic design by Scott Arany

BLACK FOREST

A novel by Valérie Mréjen

Translated from the French
by Katie Shireen Assef

Deep Vellum Publishing
Dallas, Texas

A MAN IS AT HOME ONE AFTERNOON. He attempts to carry out a number of actions in a particular order, focusing on their progress. His gaze is drawn to the window overlooking the street and he takes in the people coming and going, their shoulders pulled down by various weights: bags of all sizes, overcoats, trenches. Legs carry these bodies composed and comprised of organs, some of which function better than others; legs continuously cross paths, legs march on; heads nod, ruminating over a thousand disparate things, and hair swings forward and back. Anonymous heads of hair shine in the pale, cold light of the winter sun, curling, lifting in cowlicks, fading, and becoming streaked with white strands—just a few at first, then many, if only they're given the time and the chance.

The man in the apartment decides he is old enough. He takes the disco ball down from its beam and in its place ties a rope, which he likely found in the hardware section of the bric-a-brac shop not far from his building. He loops it around his neck and, standing on the stepladder, now observes the room from high up.

Something startles the downstairs neighbors—a noise like metal hitting a concrete floor—and they freeze.

ON ONE DECEMBER 31ST, THIS man's birthday, a family is getting ready for a New Year's Eve party. The divorced father will be bringing his three children to the house of a friend of their stepmother's. They won't know anyone there and fear they'll be terribly bored. In a lavish apartment resembling the set of a TV movie, a young, newly-hired maid will have tried to add a festive touch to the decor by placing tiny baskets of artificial flowers on tablecloths that will give the hosts a reason to recount their lengthy bargaining sessions at markets in poor countries. The absurdly low price that had been obtained through persistence will be brandished like a victory. Yet, considering the ugliness of the spoils, it will seem still too much to the eldest child, a nervous, aloof teenager who feels uneasy in this company.

Before heading out to the party, the family must change into nicer clothes. The outfits chosen by the youngest two aren't chic enough: they didn't bring with them any perfectly ironed new shirts, nor flannel trousers or little English blazers. They do not, for that matter, own such clothing, since their father hates spending Saturdays at department stores and doesn't know of any other, more fashionable places to shop. Every now and again, he takes them to an obscure boutique in the wholesale district, where a man who smells of eau de toilette and claims to have known them since they were babies makes them try on parkas too poorly cut to look like the ones in the window display, and knockoff shoes modeled after the latest styles. They don't dare object, and the fitting is always an ordeal. They leave with pleated pants made of itchy fabric that zip so tightly they can hardly breathe, all rolled up into plastic bags whose rigid snap-seals never close completely and whose sharp-edged handles leave red and white marks on their palms.

And so it is decided that they will stop by their mother's. She's out of town for the weekend with her lover—this is how the father refers to this man he's never met, lover, though the divorce was finalized years ago and he, too, is involved with someone new. The father has a friend; the mother sees her lover. The family drives down deserted alleys lit by gas lamps, through a wealthy neighborhood where the broad avenues are lined with hundred-year-old chestnut trees, to a duller suburb full of one-way streets. The car pulls up in front of a duplex and the children are asked to hurry, or so they gather from their father's exaggerated sigh. The brother begins to insert his key into the star-shaped keyhole and senses, from the absence of pressure, that the door isn't locked. Someone has been here before them. There's a light on in the kitchen; the warm halo of recently installed sconces has been illuminating the white wall for several hours. On the tiled floor, they see the pieces of a broken plate.

They call out, wait for a response, and climb the first flight of stairs; they understand, of course, that none of this is normal. In the room at the end of the hallway, a presence awaits them: a woman who looks exactly like their mother, in a state resembling sleep, lies in a nightgown under the covers. They recognize the fake fur bedspread, the two antique nightstands perched on slender, graceful feet, the mysterious marquetry drawers inside which they've always hoped to find a surprise and instead only come upon little ivory or burlwood boxes containing their yellowed baby teeth split neatly in halves, or an old sewing kit—things already familiar to them. On the pillow, the waxy face appears calm, the half-closed eyes pointed toward a spot on the ceiling.

THE FAMILY WILL TRY TO make sense of what has happened, unable to stop themselves from asking the same questions over and over as if, given enough time, a clear explanation might by some miracle occur to them and make it all seem a little more logical. Why did this thirty-eight-year-old woman and mother of three, enamored with her new boyfriend, come home early from her romantic weekend away? The boyfriend will say he doesn't know, that he honestly has no idea. Nothing had happened between them that could have made her decide to return home that night. Maybe he'd unknowingly said something that hurt her. Maybe he'd said something *to* hurt her, partly on purpose. Maybe, in taking a valiant stab at complete sincerity, he'd been too harsh with her. Maybe he'd hoped to strengthen their bond by making a carefully worded observation, or tried to express his frustration with one or another of her neuroses, taking for granted her ability to handle criticism. Maybe he'd been cruel to her out of exhaustion, out of impatience. Maybe he had wanted to rile her a little.

The fact remains that she took the pills. On the staircase, the dark blue, almost black uniforms and helmets of the police who have come to confirm the death make the event seem strangely official. Their colleagues at the station must be waiting for them, planning to open a bottle of champagne at midnight. At midnight, the officers on duty at the neighborhood precinct will clink their glasses, call their wives, children, parents, and will all wish each other a happy 1986. For the time being, they go about their work in the suburbs: at the end of a cul-de-sac overgrown with rosebushes and in the midst of a family no longer in a holiday mood, they watch as young children faint at the sight of a dead body.

SOMEWHERE IN PARIS, IN A sparsely furnished studio apartment, two police officers come to the aid of a woman lying on a mattress on the floor. They turn her on her side, clumsily manipulating the soft, inert mass that has just ejected a spurt of liquid from its mouth. The woman's partner, who called them here, says that she takes barbiturates every day, sometimes five or six in the early evening when she's feeling depressed. A doctor in a white coat arrives, throws a startled glance at the man filming the scene, and promptly kneels at the ailing woman's bedside. A nurse is there, too, falling into step behind him. The partner stays on the landing with the officers, one of whom—young and mustached—says the word *asphyxiation*, trying to downplay the situation. He repeats once or twice that *it was a close call*. In the very next shot, slightly further down the staircase, the young doctor can be seen taking the man gently by the arm and pulling him aside.

AT THE MOMENT WHEN THE siblings flee the house in total panic to alert their father, who takes an eternity to extract himself from the car, wanting to know first what all the fuss is about and repeating "what? what is it," demanding a good reason to unfold his body from the car seat and stop vaguely musing on the drabness of the street, where perhaps a bundled-up grannie is lingering—at this moment that seems unending to the children, the moment when they are faced with the obstinacy of their father who sits there sunken like an enormous stone in the leather seat—at that moment, their older sister leaves a flashy, overpriced hair salon near Pont d'Iéna with her stepmother, who'd insisted they both get a cut and blow-dry *à l'américaine*. The hour or more she had spent in that place—where she disliked every single thing, where the heady, musky air was like cloying perfume and rich women pouted like imperious children—only widens the unbearable gap between these two nearly simultaneous events: her siblings' encounter with a stiff corpse in the house from which they will now have to move, and the teasing of her hair with round brushes and aerosol spray in a place where conversations are so empty that the whir of blow-dryers is almost a blessing.

SHE MUST HAVE FOUND OUT shortly after everyone else, calling her mother's house at the prompting of the stunned housekeeper, who had also just heard the news in this way. Her brother had answered the phone, but could only hand the receiver over to their father, who, for his part, knew no other way than to get right to the point, announcing it flatly and finally. The absurd sophistication of her hairstyle, like an old bourgeois lady's, made her feel as if she'd been dropped into a bad soap opera—so often had she watched and re-watched those lion-maned actresses reacting to bad news over the telephone—and not long after, she went to another hairdresser more suited to her style and age, and had her head completely shaved.

How do we take up this conversation where we'd left it? With what words should we begin? No doubt with the usual *how are you*, even if it rings hollow.

If the young and stylish woman had been in less of a hurry after work, then she might have taken the time to read the warning label on the device before installing it. She might have studied the instructions in the language of her choice, and placed an alarm at her side before undressing. And then she might not have fallen so soundly asleep—tired at the end of a long day and with no vacation in sight—after plugging in the neon lights, allowing the ultraviolet rays to scorch her skin as she slept. She won't sun herself on any wide beaches this summer, since she'll have been burned to death without knowing it, between the walls of a device that had arrived in a cardboard box, in an apartment that will likely be packed up into a few suitcases when they come to empty the premises.

I reached, then surpassed, the age she was when she died, and now find myself in the strange position of having become her elder. When I crossed this threshold I told myself that any person in my situation must experience more or less the same thing: the fear of being struck down at once, an unusually pronounced sense of guilt, and at the same time, a kind of relief.

IN A SUNNY REGION OF the country, several married couples, a few of them with children, are summering together in a villa with a swimming pool. One night, two young children, a brother and sister, quietly leave their beds, walk down the stairs and out into the darkened garden and tread over the cool grass toward the pool, entranced by the luminescent turquoise of the water. At sunrise, when the children don't answer a few calls from inside the house, the adults go out looking for them and find them drowned, floating on the surface of the pool. The women immediately take the bereaved mother into their care, staying with her in the house and attending to a few of the practical matters, while the men head to the station to meet the children's father, who will arrive later in the day. As he waits to disembark the train, he spots his friends at the edge of the platform and wonders why so many of them have come, why this entire delegation, and understands, then, without a word, that something unusual must have happened.

ONE NIGHT, I DREAM SHE is living in Nanterre. Why this city, I wonder. Like a detective in a film noir who frowns and mumbles the same enigmatic phrase several times in the hope of a revelation, I hear myself pronouncing *n'enterre*, the negation of *enterre*—bury—again and again. In the same dream, she is passing through Rome, which sounds like *mort* backwards.

She wears a sun hat over very long hair. She grows organic vegetables. I find her utterly New Age.

AND IF THIS OTHER WOMAN—AN acquaintance of distant acquaintances, the connections so garbled in the passage from mouth to mouth that nobody knows who really knew her anymore—if only this woman hadn't laughed so heartily at the anecdote she'd heard from a fellow guest at a sauerkraut party. If she hadn't leaned backward and caused her larynx to dilate, so that she risked aspirating a piece of food. If the guest had embellished his story a bit so as to draw out the jovial mood, or had been interrupted, or paused to serve himself another spoonful or two; if he'd been slowed by a coughing fit, or if his phone had vibrated and he'd pulled it out of his pocket, and glanced, with some annoyance, at the name of her potential savior, even if he'd decided not to answer it before delivering his punch line; a few seconds would have sufficed, and this poor soul would have been able to chew her piece of sausage.

WHAT NEWS IS THERE TO tell after twenty-five years? The Printemps department store is still here. The Grands Boulevards, too. The retailer across the street that used to sell such typically British products has closed for good, having failed to make enough profit in France. Too few people here cared to buy floral pajamas or ruffled blouses. It's unfortunate, but I'll admit I didn't shop there much, either. That said, it's now easy to get to London by train through a tunnel that runs beneath the English Channel. She must have gone to England for a language study trip sometime before she was married. I know she traveled to Germany, to the Black Forest and Baden-Baden, where as a child she accompanied her mother to thermal spa hotels; to Italy, a little seaside town in the Province of Rimini, several summers in a row; to Morocco for her honeymoon; and to Switzerland for winter sports.

Metro and bus tickets have gone from yellow to blue-green to purple to monogrammed white. The currency has changed, and the tables in certain cafés now double as advertising spaces (a round poster, warped by humidity, is glued to the bottom of a hollow tabletop). There is an Opera Bastille, a Louvre pyramid, a new district near the Seine, a vast national library, bicycles to rent at self-service stations.

The year 2000, which everyone had thought of as a kind of science-fictional future, is already far behind us, and despite all the talk of a fatal catastrophe, we entered this decade with relative smoothness. The calculations we made then to determine how old we would be proved correct in my case, and from that moment on, the logos and labels associated with the number 2000 felt oddly dated, as if the magnetic needle used to predict trends had suddenly switched over to point toward the past.

SHE WOULD FEEL LIKE A foreigner. Against my better judg-
ment, l sometimes catch myself dreaming of her sudden reap-
pearance, and of what an adventure it would be to stroll with
her through the streets of Paris. Everything would prove a
source of astonishment: people walking while talking on cell
phones, some with invisible earpieces, would look to her like
fools chattering endlessly to themselves; at first her reactions
would amuse me, but soon enough I'd grow impatient and
raise my eyebrows with a touch of affectionate irony, as you
do with a small-town cousin who is easily impressed by the
big city, as if this whole dense and mechanized environment
were our personal achievement, a phenomenal sequence of
modern engines designed and assembled expressly to daz-
zle him. Everything would seem alien to her: the passersby
rushing about; the plane trees with their camouflage-pat-
terned bark; the fluttering of leaves in the wind; her ability
to once again read facial expressions and the posters at bus
stops—a thousand details would bring her to a halt and tell
her something about the present day. I'd feel as if l were
dragging along a child who'd just woken up from a two-de-
cade-long nap. She would diligently name each object as if to
assure herself that she remembered it, or perhaps to feel, in
pronouncing each word, the euphoria of being reunited with
the elements of this world. Since she no longer had any destination, she'd dawdle and inevitably annoy the more hurried
pedestrians. As for those who would groan in frustration—

striding purposefully past us while a few snatches of their insults cut through the street noises to fall on my ears—I would curse their rudeness and have to restrain myself from lecturing them for daring to betray a spasm of exasperation. I would be convinced I'd brushed shoulders with brutes, with monsters who'd go to any lengths to be on time, willing to push half the world aside. I'd denounce their crass behavior, though I never fail to do the same whenever a lone miserable ambler has the gall to slow me down with his snail's pace, and what's more, to stand right in the middle of the sidewalk. I'd hold her arm as though she were a timid fiancée and walk with her into the crowd, scanning the eyes of passersby for signs of surprise at the sight of us, as if the whole world must have known her; and I'd wonder, secretly, if they thought we were sisters. Just as when you go out for the first time with a new hairstyle, I'd feel vaguely disappointed at the absence, however ordinary, of any reactions around us.

I'd look both ways several times at street corners, putting the oft-repeated counsel into practice with new zeal. The neighborhood I am sometimes so bored of walking in would seem to me a curious maze of enticing window displays, and the shops selling ornate faux-antique metal candlesticks and picture frames for farewell gifts or over-the-hill parties would lure us in and, who knows, maybe even sell us something. She might not have fully regained her critical faculties and have lost the ability to detect ugliness in certain objects.

With a twinge of embarrassment, I picture her lingering, for example, between a cheetah-skin rug and a gilded rhinoceros, in awe of the too-shiny marble and crystal furnishings under the spotlights of a boutique lined with mirrors. What I'd want to show her—what, for my part, I'd think worthy of her attention—wouldn't interest her, and her eye would stray to details that held no meaning for me. I'd insist on bringing her to a café in my neighborhood where I sometimes meet those friends I sense will be partial to this slightly dated and preserved islet; run by a perfectly Chabrolian woman who is always elegant and smartly dressed, her jet-black hair pinned up in a chignon, her full bosom protruding beneath a crepe blouse where a cut-glass pendant swings at the end of a gold chain, the place is calm and secluded, brimming with bouquets all year long. It's reminiscent of a country hotel, and small enough that the arrival of a new customer, announced by the softest chiming of bells, is always considered an event. A precious silence reigns there, precious when you're used to the soundtrack of the street: buses, trucks, heavy-duty trucks, cars, scooters, bicycles (electric or not), delivery vans, minivans, motorcycles, mopeds, strollers (motorized or not), roller skaters, skateboarders, pedestrians in pumps or in flat-heeled shoes. But the almost religious tranquility of the place, and the presence of all these cut flowers fated to wilt in a few days' time, would have for her an air of déjà vu, and nothing more.

AFTER THE 2004 TSUNAMI, THE name of a blue-eyed woman, referred to by her family as "our sunshine," is printed in the missing persons column of a daily newspaper. She'd been spending her Christmas vacation on the coast of one of the countries where the disaster struck. The notice does not speculate, only reports a concern, barely alluding to an eventuality no one wants to acknowledge, for they all continue to hope. But soon they can't stop themselves from stringing together and reiterating a chain of theories that drive one another out, narrowing the possibilities (roughly the same for most everyone stunned by this news): she would have called her daughter. She would've sent her a text message, even a short one. She would've borrowed a phone if her own had sunk into the murky water filled with corpses and debris. She would've found a hotel to call from, or asked someone else to call; she would certainly have found a way to reach her. She must be wounded, or unconscious, or paralyzed. Lying on a stretcher, emptied of strength and courage, she can neither carry out this task nor make herself understood in English. She probably has no paper or pencil, no way of communicating the number and area code. All the lines are surely down or busy. But as the days go by, these theories invented to keep hope alive are exhausted, one after another.

A BURNING SMELL DRIFTS INTO the apartment, seemingly coming from the floor above. She goes upstairs and finds herself on her neighbor's landing; thick gray plumes of smoke billow out from under the door. She hears a loud noise from inside and knocks, wondering if anyone is even there. A student, visibly disturbed and in the throes of a breakdown, opens the door to a disheveled room, at the center of which can be seen, on the floor, a pile of blazing papers and objects. In an instinct of self-preservation, she yells at him to put out the fire. Everything happens quickly: the young man grabs a knife and stabs this woman of nearly forty, admired by her colleagues, loved by her family, the mother of two young children. Downstairs in their apartment, her husband, worried by the length of her absence, rushes up to meet her and finds her covered in blood, already in agony. She expires in his arms while her murderer leaps out the window and falls seven stories to his death.

WE WOULD LEAVE THIS CHARMING place, and probably for the best since, truth be told, I don't know what she would've ordered. We rarely ever went out to cafés or, rather, it was so long ago I have no memory of her taste.

We clearly wouldn't know how to begin again. I'd be afraid of seeming hurried, of sharing needless information, of trying to make up for lost time by talking far too much, inevitably marring this fantasy reunion.

ANOTHER DREAM: WE'RE RIDING ALONG the highway in a minivan, an *Espace* model, in the company of two married friends. The husband, Bob, is an old man now but livelier and more enthusiastic than most young people, which fills those around him with a kind of envious admiration.

Still, we're a bit more apprehensive each time we ask him how he's been, and it's hard not to think of the day when he *won't* be doing so well—as he himself does, for that matter, with blunt pragmatism and a passionate hatred of all sentimentality.

He shrinks from the gestures of affection, from the excessive politeness and sympathy of strong, robust, well-meaning people who tilt their head to the side when they listen to him or offer him their arm on the staircase. When we ask after his health, his wife's cheerful response is always a relief, a temporary victory over fate. He'd been an eminent cancer specialist before he was forced into retirement, and had too often rubbed shoulders with death throughout his life to be truly afraid of it.

In my dream, as the car continues along the highway, we try to recall the title of a Lubitsch film. It's never the right one; again and again we think we have it, but keep grasping to no avail. I suggest *The Shop Around the Corne*r, *Ninotchka,* and others, but the one we're trying to name eludes us, and it's terribly frustrating. Bob and his wife are not really cinephiles and I'm surprised to find myself carrying on this conversation with them. In the end, I fail to come up with the answer to our riddle. On waking, I go to look up the filmography of the prince of comedy: it was *Heaven Can Wait*.

I COULD BEGIN HERE, AND use this story as a way to start the conversation, adding as an aside that heaven could, in effect, have waited a little longer, that it's a shame to have gone so soon. I'd try and make a simple declaration—*I've missed you* for instance—but such a common turn of phrase as this would seem all wrong. And then the words would remain stuck, unable to emerge from the depths of my throat, trapped by vocal cords that are suddenly stiff and swollen and exude bitter bile from the same place where a knot forms, every so often, whenever I happen to say "my mother."

I WOULD START AGAIN FROM the beginning: Le Printemps still exists, the Carte Orange pass has disappeared; her father died alone, leaving behind a few debts and four grandchildren; the neighborhood beyond the boulevard Périphérique, where we used to live, has expanded and now consists mainly of towers and office buildings. We sold the house that we'd bought on a twenty-year loan, which was paid off by the insurance.

ONCE HER AMAZEMENT AT THE offerings in the decor shops had passed, and her powers of discernment kicked in again, she'd no doubt be appalled by certain aspects of the present; in the first place, the way people have of proudly rallying behind the respected—and even feared—cult of the *carefree*. Having attached so much importance to decency and discretion, she'd feel taken aback by a certain pervading boorishness.

Of course, we could dream of joining this club and of finally throwing off our chains, the limitations, real or imagined, that have set up shop in our subconscious whether we like it or not. I know of many people who would make ideal members and yet who don't dare apply, for fear of being deemed unfit—and even so, given the chance, not only would they readily empty their wallets, they'd also find the membership fees too low. One, an intelligent, sensitive, erudite man, believes he's useless and will say as much to whoever will listen, and in truth, to himself most of all. Another, a gorgeous, exuberantly funny woman, sees herself a bumbling moron and looks aghast as soon as she opens her mouth, convinced she's let slip an uncouth remark that's bound to reveal her stupidity. The minute she returns home from a dinner party, she sends out messages apologizing for all the nonsense she spoke. Yet another, gifted, charming, putting her talents to work at a prestigious organization, has lived for years with an inexplicably arrogant deadbeat, and ended up believing, like him, that she really can't be taken anywhere. What's more, she often tells friends who adore her that she'd rather avoid giving her own opinion, since it isn't worth much. As for the man—who has no qualms about living under her roof and off her paycheck—he approves of this restraint, and strongly encourages it. For once, he thinks, she's got it right.

It must be a relief to finally find a way to feel more confident, to move through life unfettered by self-doubt, to stop tormenting yourself with the need to justify even the smallest action. But this is not what is meant by 'being carefree'; in fact, it is quite the opposite. You must proclaim your flaws as virtues—as priceless advantages, even—and if only by starting to believe as much, obstinately and without further delay. I don't think she'd understand this peculiar new trend.

THE MAN IN THAT SCENE in Raymond Depardon's *Faits divers* has no time to grasp the situation: the woman stretched out beside him on the thin mattress on the floor who looks as if she's sleeping and has taken barbiturates, simply exceeded her usual dose and passed away in her sleep. Everything in the small room is evocative of the 1980s: the photo of the Eiffel Tower, the tabletop on trestle legs, the clip-on lamp with its adjustable arm, prints of famous paintings and movie posters, everyday objects typical of that time. There's a slightly rancid odor that must penetrate your nostrils on first walking in the door—

a whiff of congealed sweat, old laundry, scalps grimy with pollution, rugs that ought to be shaken out, kitchen fumes that have permanently impregnated the walls—then gradually dissipate after a time spent in the room.

The officer asks if they were married and the man begins to say that they were about to be, that they'd prepared the documents, and then bursts into tears again, understanding, afresh, what has just happened. In the course of the weeks to come, he'll be brutally confronted with the event in more ways still: through persistent logical deadlocks, the need to cancel plans, the sporadic and totally unpredictable arrival of promotional offers from a coupon service, which he won't have the courage to throw away and whose subscription he will, bizarrely, be even less capable of canceling. This is why he'll sometimes dread opening his mailbox: for fear of finding brightly colored brochures promising discounts on window installations, or on eyeglass frames she'd never needed in her lifetime—not at her age, anyway.

AFTER RETURNING HOME FROM A weekend by the sea with her son and grandchildren, a woman enters a strange state that somewhat troubles those close to her, even if it doesn't appear all that serious. From the outside, the situation might seem comical: halfway through a lucid sentence, she will drift off into what sounds like nonsense. When the symptoms persist and begin to prove worrisome, her sister ends up calling a doctor to the house. Soon brothers and cousins are exchanging phone calls and updates in tones already solemn, if still incredulous.

They suggest she consent to a few examinations, and the moment she steps through the doors of the hospital, her condition transforms irreversibly into a *condition*. She starts babbling, and her loved ones use the expression "in her own world" to try and make sense of this inexplicable phenomenon. It's soon found to be a matter of a sodium deficiency, as though the woman had been absorbing liters of water without consuming enough salt, which is odd, since she salts her food generously and doesn't drink enough fluids. This explanation seems misplaced and it's difficult to understand how a sodium deficiency no one had been aware of could make her talk gibberish, or call her sons several times in a row just to confirm that she has their numbers, as if she were a screwball character in one of those zany comic strips in waiting room magazines.

The doctors learn nothing from the X-rays or her other test results, and the family decides that this must be normal, a sign that the state of confusion is passing or had been aggravated by the hospital setting itself. Though the details that the medical staff gradually delivers are baffling to the uninitiated, they nonetheless circulate, phone call by phone call, as the hours wear on, and whenever a new term is introduced, those who hear it first do their best to explain it to the others.

Finally, the diagnosis is made, and everyone takes a moment to grasp that the illness, alluded to by an unfamiliar euphemism or another inscrutable phrase, is very grave indeed, and well known to them all. And from that point on she deteriorates rapidly: the cycle of treatments exhausts her, her hair falls out, morale weakens, and the uncontrollable, nervous laughter that erupts between brothers quickly gives way to tears. They cling to what they can and try to find in all of this some incongruity or odd detail that, under the circumstances, triggers fits of wild hilarity—the "as seen on TV" sticker on the window of a funeral home or an employee's garish necktie become irresistible fodder for jokes among family members.

The two adult sons have occasional panic attacks and experience strange somatic symptoms that appear out of nowhere, sensory malfunctions and other disturbances which, after medical consultation, seem to also stem from a kind of anxiety.

To HELP FIGHT OFF THIS malaise, the younger brother's wife takes him by the hand and leads him outside for a walk along the streets. It will do them good, she says, and it's better not to stay holed up. They walk across Paris, on this morning a palette of grays: the nearly black lead of the asphalt, the dark granite of the lumpy cobblestones covered in dust, the dull flannel edges of the sidewalks, the raw steel of the sky's reflection in the gutter water, the walls of adjoined buildings along the Hausmannian boulevards, zinc rooftops stained blue-gray by the rain. They cross the Seine, whose restless surface adds a splash of beige to this otherwise monochromatic landscape, and their footsteps lead them to the boulevard de l'Hôpital. At the little zoo in the Jardin des Plantes, yellow and ultramarine frogs with tiny, suckered feet are kept in aquariums that have been heated to simulate their home climate. A panel explains that they are highly toxic and that contact with their skin can be fatal. Certain species had been confiscated at customs when traffickers tried to smuggle them into our country.

They eagerly observe these little beings, so very different from themselves, as they move around and breathe behind each window of the vivarium. There are stick insects that resemble fallen leaves, snakes with fixed, sidelong gazes that look sinister even if they turn out not to be poisonous and whose scales appear incredibly delicate and strange; it's delightful and astonishing to see these odd, lithe specimens moving almost imperceptibly along a crooked liana vine. They watch as immense tortoises, some over a hundred years old, drag their massive shells like bronze armor and laboriously raise their clawed, leathery feet, stretching their wrinkled necks toward the water of the sunken pond they've known all their lives. The couple is enchanted by the sudden strangeness and novelty of nature, as if discovering these animals for the first time; by the insects' whimsical bodies in the shape of twigs or lengths of string; by the dangerous, nearly fluorescent amphibians; by the giant reptiles from the Galapagos Islands that they call prehistoric, for want of a better term.

They pause for a moment before an enormous, bright green iguana who emphatically ignores them. The animal crouches sideways, head high, crest erect, hooked claws gripping a branch. They marvel at his eye, no bigger than the head of a pin, set in the tip of a cone-shaped eyelid, his skin as rumpled as the folds of a toga. His fat, drooping belly and the multiple creases under his chin are markers of a certain age, and his self-important air distinguishes him from the other creatures of whom he clearly considers himself the king. He keeps still as a statue, indifferent to his two attentive visitors, though they've been watching him for some time now. Suddenly, he decides to change position, but he loses his balance and his foot slips down: stiff with fright at the edge of an abyss, he somehow straightens himself to keep from falling, at the same time releasing a trickle of urine that completely soaks the rare vegetation at the base of his habitat. The scene could be called "Grandeur and Degradation," so quickly has the poor fellow gone from one state to another, having simply wanted to move a few centimeters to the left.

The vivarium is terribly old and charming with its checkered mosaic of 1930s tiles, a low ceiling and round pillars of rugged concrete, with footsteps that resound on the floor, grinding bits of loose gravel carried in on the soles of shoes, and words that amplify and blend together in an echo like the hubbub that rises from school courtyards. The sight of each new cage fills them with a mix of curiosity and apprehension before they discover which creature it houses.

Farther on, the couple is captivated by the orangutans: a young one, in particular, nestling at its mother's breast, with eyes round as marbles set in a wrinkled face, a tuft of ginger hair planted on the very top of its head. It's the first time they can remember watching animals so closely and they feel at ease in this place, among creatures who are born and die in their own way, who survive, perish, form clans, and care for their young before finally releasing them into the wild—not here, of course, but in theory.

HIS SON AND DAUGHTER ARE grown. Long divorced, he lives like a bachelor in a small apartment bought with his inheritance, the largest room of which serves as a studio. For years he's continued to paint in his free time, despite an almost total absence of visibility and recognition. Though relatively open minded, he's always been a bit conservative when it comes to art history and never once questioned the traditional instruction he likely received in his small coastal town. To his mind, painting alone is noble, with oils preferably, and in a figurative style or at least one that depicts an easily recognizable subject. Rather than expose them to the world's pitiless gaze, he prefers to remain in seclusion with his canvases, smoking blond-tobacco cigarettes and drinking wine; that is, except for once or twice a year when the studios in his neighborhood open their doors and a few friends and neighbors come by to chat, helping themselves to crackers from an old ceramic bowl and admiring the passageways normally closed to the public, the ivy-covered walls of buildings in this corner of Paris. Who'd have known such charming places still exist—all you have to do is open a door to find yourself in another world, you'd almost think you were in the countryside. It's so very agreeable. Have you lived here long? Do you rent or own? It must be very expensive now. You're lucky to have bought at the right time. It's impossible to find such places these days; people form networks and let their neighbors know even before they post an ad, or else you have to be friendly with the concierge.

He paints ectoplasmic bodies, gauzy, granular ghosts floating in tangled masses against black backgrounds. One day in his room, he sits up in bed, leans his head against the wall, and looks out the window facing a small courtyard. His son, worried when he doesn't respond to a text message suggesting they go out for a picnic, stops by to visit, and finds him in this position.

HE BROUGHT HIS THREE CHILDREN to a faraway coast for their summer vacation, leaving his new partner, who isn't a full-fledged member of the family yet, in Paris. His loved ones don't seem to have been too upset by his change in sexual orientation, and he's maintained a good rapport with his ex-wife. Since he met the man of his life, both are radiant, joyful, fulfilled. Their friends are convinced they were destined to find each another.

It's the end of summer, that last week in August when pictures of crowded beaches begin dissolving into images of leaves falling onto squares and avenues. It's still a bit early to call: people might not be home yet, some take only a few days off, and those who stay in the city prefer to keep a low profile and make the most of the calm before their first engagements. Still, the news makes its way around their small circle of friends within just a few hours: there, in that country, driving with his children in a rented car through a place he knew a little, but not well enough to navigate the roads with ease, he found himself in the middle of a neighborhood like so many others, with nearly identical high-rise buildings and narrow alleyways, at the hottest hour of the afternoon—there, he must have taken a wrong turn on a one-way street and crashed into a car coming from the opposite direction. His life was extinguished in that fraction of a second, at the moment when a red and white road sign failed to catch his eye.

Those of us close to his new partner ask ourselves how we can be of help, what words of consolation to offer, what pitiful twig we can add to the dam we'd like to build—in vain, we know—against a tidal wave of grief whose force necessarily escapes us. Probably the best we can do is to send the occasional sign that we're there for him, and hope that in time his pain will begin to recede, that he will, eventually, find some respite from it.

THEY'VE JUST MOVED INTO A rental apartment on the corner of a boulevard, right above a bakery, and since it's on the second floor, part of their living room can be glimpsed through the windows as night falls. Neither one has really let go of their old love, which complicates their already stormy relationship, laden with a certain tension; their evenings are occasionally ruined by fierce arguments, though in the morning everything is always better again. With his slightly rugged appearance and faux bad-boy air, with the deep crease between his eyebrows and his fingers gnarled by manual work, you'd never think he could make such delicate jewelry. You'd never guess that a man like him—in a black leather jacket, on a roaring motorcycle—would have silver ingots and curved pincers in his tail box, or that he'd use them to make chain-linked rings with polished stones in clusters that fall nonchalantly to this side or that, depending on the movement of the hand wearing them. When they'd first met, some months ago, she was still living with her long-time boyfriend, the childhood companion with whom she shared so many memories, their photographs tucked away in shoeboxes that had moved with them several times already. Then, after this childhood friend had sanctioned their breakup by pursuing a new lover of his own, the biker-jeweler had sprinkled a few handfuls of gold powder along the sidewalk in front of their building, as if rolling out a path to her little room, drawing a shining trail in the light of the streetlamps so that she had only to follow, leaving her precious footprints behind in the pulverized metal.

She'd finally moved in with him, but the loss was fresh and she kept a few of the shoeboxes filled with photos of her former life, photos in which the couple's still childlike faces could be seen surrounded by friends: there was a black-and-white series of her in the early morning, sitting before an old coffee service and a vase of hyacinths; a windowed ceiling framed against the light; colored photo booth snapshots where he had close-cropped hair and wore a plaid shirt; and yellowed polaroids from their somewhat hippie period, the young lovers in tunics and embroidered slippers picnicking near a fountain in a large Indian city to which they had returned several times; or else in the courtyard of their first building, repairing a bicycle or sanding shelves.

In this new apartment above the bakery, dinners are held under the pretense that nothing has changed, and by all appearances the couple is on good terms with the ex-partner, who brings with him his new fiancée and their friends from the travel photos.

At the dawn of the new year, after the whole group has spent the holidays together—not without a few minor clashes caused by a persistent twinge of jealousy—the biker-jeweler rides his motorcycle down a busy boulevard in Paris, angry and probably speeding. In the hospital of the outer suburb where a few loved ones are summoned after the accident, a tall black nurse who feels sorry for these people and wishes he could tell them something different, shakes his head with a look of utter helplessness and repeats *I don't have good news, I don't have good news.* Many years later, for those friends who are still here and whose features have inexorably slackened in the group portraits—even if the digital photos always turn out nicer—the boulevard Magenta remains permanently marked, as other places are for other people, whether a particular city square or terrace, haunted forever by he who is absent because that was the last place where he was alive.

THE SAME COULD BE SAID of the Pont Henri-IV, where a young actor of North African descent who'd grown up in Aubervilliers collided with a streetlamp: at that intersection where cars approach from the boulevard Saint-Germain while a traffic light stops those coming from the other direction, and where the sidewalk is elevated. Not far from the square where they'd shot a farewell scene in his very first film.

WE WOULD LEAVE THIS FLOWER-FILLED café and wander the streets of the neighborhood in search of another, but none would really do. I wouldn't want to take her to some awful spot where the television is on and the bar crowded with regulars, even less to an American chain serving vanilla-flavored lattes with caramel and too much foam and warnings not to burn yourself printed on the paper cups. Truth be told, no place would seem good enough to me; I'd find them all filthy and decrepit, or else pretentious and too new; empty and drab, or raucous and rowdy. In the traditional cafés, the clamor of saucers carelessly piled up and the thump, thump of espresso handles hitting the edge of a drawer would be almost unbearable to her ears, and, in the end, we'd settle on a bench in a public square. The beds of hydrangeas would remind her, curiously, of the tiny garden plot behind the suburban house where we'd lived only a few months, just long enough to renovate it—a garden so narrow and hedged in by concrete slabs that you wondered if its dense, stony earth was really from there, originally, or if it had been brought in bags and packed in layers just thick enough to nourish a few obliging plants. We'd observe the comings and goings: a group of teenagers in tracksuits lounging on the steps as if they were in their own living rooms; one or two mysterious people with seemingly no other afternoon plans than to sit alone for a while in this fairly animated place to put off growing depressed at home; toddlers fascinated by hobbling pigeons and their parents trailing behind, scolding them for trying to chase the birds or touch their feathers. We'd sit in our fenced-in islet and watch the action unfolding around us to the rhythm of the slamming and creaking of battered iron gates that visitors released behind them with a vigor that quickly dwindled into a loose swinging of arms, oblivious to the deafening noise they'd caused.

THE SEVEN-AND-A-HALF-YEAR-OLD GIRL—AND she's more than a little proud to have reached the age of reason, even if the meaning of these words remains quite obscure; it has a nice ring to it, like a victory achieved simply through the accumulation of years—the seven-and-a-half-year-old girl nurtures a kind of pure admiration. If you were to ask her *do you have a role model*, she'd be tempted to tell you and yet a little afraid to speak frankly, since her fascination might be cause for ridicule: to her it seems a bit compromising to admire one's parents so much. The connection is too obvious, the proximity embarrassing; how simple it must seem of her to have chosen as if at random these people whom fate had, in any case, placed among her forebears. She finds her mother almost intimidating, strangely out of reach—maybe it's because of her black hair, jet black, as she's often heard it described, the same words that are used in *Snow White*: the young princess of legendary beauty has black hair, as black as jet or ebony, and these two rare materials which she knows only by name seem equally wonderful to her. Her mother is Snow White, a naïvely charming, innocent girl, banished by an evil queen who is none other than her own aging and jealous stepmother, and who worries—not without reason—that her stepdaughter's beauty might charm her third husband. And so the queen decides to marry her off without further delay: soon the engagement is announced, then the wedding, and finally, the birth of this little girl who admires her so.

The child wants so much to be like her mother that one day she decides to imitate her as closely as possible, to follow her everywhere and mimic her gestures in perfect synchrony. She pursues her frantically through the rooms of the apartment, runs after her into the bathroom to copy her morning routine, trails her like a shadow in the hallway, the floorboards groaning horribly despite endless precautions and betraying her presence even on tiptoe; she stays close on her heels, relentless, trying to mirror her every movement with absolute precision, clearly intent on becoming a sort of twin, on achieving as perfect a resemblance as possible. Very quickly, though, she realizes that this little lark only serves to annoy her mother, who scolds her for getting underfoot, for constantly being in the way, and in the end she's forced to accept the disheartening fact that she'll never attain the status of clone. All the same, she confesses, in a moment of cheerful forthrightness, that she'd devised this game in the hope of becoming her mother's double, and yet instead of the reaction she wishes for—involving, if not the revelation of some magical formula to help her achieve this purpose, at least a show of bemused affection—her mother sighs, impatient, and all at once the little girl is disenchanted, the echo of her words left hanging in the air.

NOW TWELVE YEARS OLD, THE girl makes up her mind one day to never again say anything at all that might elicit a look of disapproval. She mustn't say the wrong thing or speak out of turn ever again. It's devastating to hear Snow White correct her each time she misquotes something or misremembers the name of the hero in a novel, and so she resolves to read every single book in the library, under cover of night, so that she can finally reap the reward she's been dreaming of: a show of confidence, in any form, but if at all possible a litany of praises spoken before a very large audience and recorded for posterity so that she can play it over and over again, basking in the words for years to come. The girl is mortified by the condescending looks that often accompany the correction of an error. It truly is discouraging to not know everything, to not grasp certain references that might have allowed her to join in her mother's friends' conversations about the comic strips of their youth or yé-yé music. She wonders how she might secretly research these things or, at the very least, hide her ignorance (*crass ignorance* is an expression she's often heard, much like *filthy as a pigsty*) and it's only years later that she thinks back and realizes that this wasn't altogether natural, that sometimes parents teach their children a thing or two rather than always leaving them to grapple with an obsessive fear of misspeaking, of being taken for an idiot, of falling short in the eyes of the more worldly-wise.

BUT THIS IS ALL SO far in the past now that the girl, just over twenty-three, sometimes wonders if she hadn't blown things out of proportion, attaching too much meaning to nuances of speech that a less obsessive person might not even have picked up on. She understands now that the mind invests too much in certain memories, willfully fixating on this or that remark until its surplus value accrues enormously, while other phrases, spoken in kinder tones, depreciate and are in time forgotten.

HE'S A DEVOTED FAN OF *Six Feet Under*. On this day, like any other, he sits down to watch the latest episode, but the opening credits have barely begun when he starts to feel unwell.

Fade to white, shots of wilting lilies, graves marked with American names, a crow's feet gripping the edge of a head-stone: he still has a few seconds to make his way through the two-bedroom apartment and crouch over the toilet bowl to relieve himself of whatever is bloating his stomach, and so he runs into the tiny bathroom, where he feels cramped since he's recently put on quite a bit of weight—and it hits him like an avalanche. He collapses to the floor, no doubt from a heart attack, and his opulent body blocks the doorway, trapping him inside. Meanwhile, his girlfriend, in total horror, throws herself against the closed door with all her strength, pound-ing away at the oppressive silence, crying out his name.

THE CHILD HAS GROWN INTO a teenager, and the rift between the two of them has widened, her mother telling her over and over that her very presence is exasperating, that she sucks up all the air, she poisons everything, and these words are not taken lightly; the girl soon begins to see herself as a sort of thing or blob or shapeless monstrosity, something fleshy and sluggish that never fails to disgust people the moment they lay eyes on her unpleasant figure. Over time, she comes to terms with this version of things and even takes it a little further, elaborating on the idea that she is a blight on the community, picturing herself a social pariah and murmuring cruel words under her breath as if to better stoke this fierce little flame whose warmth she will almost come to appreciate.

Sitting around the large Formica table with extension flaps, a table bought at the same assemble-it-yourself furniture store as many of the other new fixtures in their home—a chain that has just opened a location on the outskirts of Paris and which people describe with excessive enthusiasm, as if it were a sign of divine providence—sitting around this smooth, white, austere table, facing a giant poster of a paradisiacal landscape bordered by groves of coconut palms, they finally decide to talk things over, to set down the facts and establish a kind of official report. They play lip-service at first, then gradually come out with the truth, each admitting how, for years now, she has seen herself through the other's eyes: a bad mother who's done so much harm that it's impossible to feel any sympathy for her, and a daughter disdained for her countless flaws and right to loathe herself.

The girl had assumed the role of the burden-arrived-too-soon, of the nuisance that kept the young princess, drawn to the freedom and audacity of the student movement in the late sixties, from thriving, never mind that she'd married before she was twenty-one and had rushed to imitate women of earlier generations, heading—just like all the bourgeois women in her family—toward a destiny that looked very much like that of a housewife. And now, fifteen years later, they decide it's time to settle their differences, to clear up the old misunderstandings; but in the end, guilt over words spoken in anger rises from one side of the table, while from the other come reassurances that all is forgiven, that there isn't a drop of resentment left. It's not worth ruining this moment since there might not be another chance, and anyway, the truth is everything will be different from now on. A drop of salt water glistens on the rim of the teenager's heavily made-up lower eyelid; she tries to delay its fall for as long as possible, but the moment she blinks it spills over the dam, a spring erupts and quickly begins to flood part of the scene, most of all the things near the Formica tabletop: a placemat of fine wooden slats held together by flexible string, which can be rolled up at the end of a meal; a pair of faded, high-waist jeans worn at the seams; a size-XL jacquard sweater that comes down to her knees to hide just how ill fitting this high-waist cut is; and a bit of crumpled paper towel that ends up looking like egg whites escaped through the crack in a shell and caught like lace in boiling water.

AS SHE STARES AT THE tropical image opposite her, the teenage girl isn't sure what to make of it, this giant poster that's nearly the same size as the ones in the metro and takes up an entire wall in their relatively small kitchen. The household is not without a sense of irony, and yet there is something oddly serious to her about this massive snapshot. It's almost as if it were being presented as a paradise at face value, and this fine sandy beach beside a lagoon with its cloudless sky and big, round sun may, after all, be the ideal horizon that sets her mother dreaming: a clichéd destination that looks a bit like something out of a travel brochure, but one she would rush off to without a second thought if someone happened to call and announce that she was the lucky winner of a week-long stay.

AFTER THE CONVERSATION IN THE kitchen facing the poster of a desert island that she could not quite picture as an Eden, so closely associated was this image with the distressing question of the famous list of books—a definitive selection, not one too many—that you'd bring to fend off boredom during a long, solitary spell (it was too risky to opt only for books you hadn't read since you might not end up liking them, but the idea of bringing books you loved and reading them over and over again until you were bored sick wasn't any more appealing); after this conversation facing the island poster, there were no more opportunities for them to grow closer. Her mother's relapse gained the upper hand, and though little by little they cut away bits of her flesh to counter the illness, it only served to confirm—following one last excision or two—just how far it had spread. The sleeping pills she took after returning home early from her weekend in the countryside only hurried things along, for she'd apparently become so fragile that the prescribed dosage she took for sleep brought her instead eternal rest. The teenager finally saw herself projected into that image, alone on an isolated beach, surrounded by waves.

SHE ATTENDS CATHOLIC SCHOOL AND lives in a residential neighborhood in a nearby suburb of Paris. On her daily walk home along shaded streets, she befriends a whimsical, outspoken girl in her grade, she who has always tended to keep in the background, preferring not to attract attention. During a class trip to England, the students who've stayed behind in France learn of her accidental death on the corner of a city street, and all they retain of the story is that the shy little girl had neglected to look in the direction from which cars never came at home, and been hit by a bus while riding her bike. There was also the image of an arm caught in the spokes of a wheel that had been described by a witness and remained frozen like a monstrous and incomprehensible collage in the mind of her boisterous best friend and neighbor, just as it did for her mother, an Englishwoman who wept bitterly over the news.

WHEN SHE DISCOVERED JACQUES BARATIER's short film *Piège*, made just before she was born, the thirty-two-year-old woman couldn't help but reflect on the connection between its two actresses, both of them filled with imagination and vitality as they run in costume through a black-and-white château and throw eggs at each other's faces. She couldn't help thinking of how these two young beauties—one blonde and the other brunette—would each lose a daughter—one brunette, the other blonde—at about the same age, under dramatic circumstances that would be reported in the newspapers.

WE'D FEEL MORE AT EASE in this tiny square than in the middle of the wide, busy thoroughfare, since here, people walk through the iron gates as if opening a parenthesis: unhurried, their gazes meandering, slowly taking each other in, acknowledging a new proximity that would give us all the false impression of having known one another, however briefly. We'd form an ephemeral group, bound merely by chance, yet nonetheless existing together at a particular moment. These faces would grow familiar in the space of an afternoon spent seated on a bench before returning to an anonymity that evoked nothing in us once we'd fallen back into the rhythm of the street, our foreheads once again furrowed with frowns, our steps hitting the pavement with determination.

ON ANOTHER DECEMBER 31ST, THE nearly forty-year-old woman receives news from Berlin that a baby has been born

and remembers that it's also the anniversary of the death
by overdose of a radio journalist she'd known, of whom it
was said, at the time, that he'd been retreating more and
more often into studio restrooms or café basements to snort
cocaine, and that the nightlife of parties and openings had
stealthily led him astray, revealing in him a certain fragility
or, perhaps, a desire for oblivion. She recalls something the
brother of this friend had written in early January, following an exchange of messages in which the word *heart* had
appeared once or twice: *it's bleeding, but it's beating.*

ONE DAY, A YEAR OR two earlier, the thirty-eight-year-old
woman accidentally came upon some letters stashed in a
drawer of her desk, an ancient roll-top secretary inherited
from her mother, while hiding her boyfriend's cigarettes to
keep him from smoking. She had to constantly change her
hiding place since he always found them in the end, whether
by turning the apartment upside down or threatening her
into confessing. This time, she'd tried to hide the pack in a
secret compartment of the old family heirloom: in addition
to the six drawers, there was an undetectable sliding panel
beneath which you could safely store a few small objects. As
she stretched out her arm toward the back of the compartment, the woman felt a stuffed, folded envelope and promptly
removed it. Inside were a dozen or so small sheets of paper,

all covered in blue ink: letters written by a certain Pierre O. (psychoanalyst, rue du Val-de-Grace), from the time when her mother had begun to question her future as a housewife and decided to "see someone", with whom she'd apparently fallen in love. The whole family thought that this correspondence, of which they'd become dimly aware in one of those hazy moments when things are guessed at without being named, had long ago been burned to ashes or torn up in an instant by the furious, jealous father. It was, in fact, at the beginning of her analysis that the mother had decided to leave him and to establish her own private practice, among other things. As she stared at the return address, the thirty-eight-year-old woman thought of a friend she'd met after high school who had lived on that same street. To confirm, she took out an old address book from another drawer and noted with astonishment that the friend in question had lived in the same building. She called her straight away to ask if she'd known this Pierre O. *But of course, of course, he was our downstairs neighbor.* This is how she learned that in those years, she had unwittingly spent hours—entire evenings—in the apartment one floor up from her mother's great forbidden love.

HE'S YOUNG, ITALIAN, AN AVID photographer, and, while on vacation, meets a Frenchman who shares this same passion. They become fast friends, keep in touch by letter and talk for hours at a time on the phone, discussing their work and their shared desire to follow an artistic path in life. They try to see each other at least once a year, when one or the other finds time to travel, but it's usually the French friend who gladly goes to spend a few days in Rome, most often in the summer. One day, he learns that his friend suffered a stroke while leaving his house, that he'd keeled over on the landing when he was on his way out to buy a loaf of bread or some other such thing.

He rides like a fiend, always gunning the engine of his huge motorcycle and trying to break his latest record. Flying down the highway one day at top speed, he loses his balance or hits an object and is dragged a great distance before he's finally catapulted like a mortar shell—the engine flying in the opposite direction—and lands, miraculously intact, in a green field of wheat. He's not dead: he manages to get up and walk, takes one step after another through the tall grass and staggers to the edge of the highway, totally disoriented by the violence of the shock. Too stunned to realize what he's doing, he begins to cross the smooth, dull strip of tarmac his footsteps seem to float over as if cushioned by a layer of cotton, freed from the effort of only a few seconds ago when his feet sank heavily into the freshly turned earth. He does not, let us hope, have time to see the truck coming.

ON RETURNING HOME FROM A trip to Peru, he starts feeling ill and decides to have a few tests done. Over there, an indigenous man had read his fortune in some coca leaves and thought he'd seen a bad omen. Now he faces therapy, radiation, an endless stream of medical charts: it's no use operating, since everyone is well aware that when the organ in question is attacked, it almost always means a fatal outcome. With what remains of his will to banter, he says of the Institut Gustave-Roussy that *it's not looking all that rosy*. He dies a few weeks later, after submitting without much conviction to the proposed care plan.

Several years ago, when he was not yet twenty, his father had suddenly vanished after taking his small boat out onto a lake. The boat had been found, as had the oars, but missing was any other evidence of his survival or death. For years it remained an unresolved tragedy: the man's wife and children, abandoned and faced with the incomprehensible, would never know what had happened. They'd make vague attempts at carrying out an investigation; they'd imagine a thousand scenarios and continue, all their lives, to wonder if the man had been kidnapped and why, or if he'd run away to begin a new life on the other side of the planet, perhaps marrying a foreigner, someone with whom he might have started a second family.

SHE'S THE SAME AGE AS my sister. Since childhood, she's taken horseback riding lessons several times a week and participated in cross-country races and obstacle courses on the weekends. The parents who accompany their children know that there are sometimes accidents; they're all too aware of the dangerousness of certain courses, and shudder before the impressive size of the fords and stone walls. Yet every Sunday, rain or shine, they wake at 5:00 or 6:00 a.m. and come in numbers to the small suburban towns, wearing raincoats and carrying cameras. She continues to practice the sport now that she's in college and, it would seem, recently engaged. During an especially arduous course, on a day when the soil is soaking wet, a poorly fixed bar falls to the ground and her horse panics: she is thrown backward into a ditch as her mount tramples her stomach, trying to escape.

SHE WAS GIVING HER BABY a bath when the landline rang; she went to answer it, leaving the child alone for a brief instant, and on returning found him lifeless, face down in the few centimeters of water that had been enough to drown him.

I DON'T KNOW IF SHE would care to hear that, years later, I met a woman with mousy gray hair, my boss, in a sense, during an internship. This woman had the ability to perfectly formulate her responses to the shoddier work we did—to correct us rigorously, but not harshly—while also possessing a kind of exuberant imagination that fascinated me and put everyone else in a carefree, jaunty mood that sometimes almost gave way to hysteria. One day, a postcard maker stopped by to sit in one of our meetings. He'd known the staff a long time and printed a whole series of cards for us to send as holiday greetings or to use as correspondence with our partners. I remember him as being in his early forties, completely independent and more or less settled in his personal and professional life, though none of this had kept him, some time earlier, from asking my boss to "adopt" him—and even before she'd had a chance to respond, he'd taken to calling her *maman*. This joke brought even more merriment to the already lighthearted office atmosphere, and in no time it was as though this new bond of parentage had been validated by the entire staff, who wouldn't miss out on a laugh for anything. I was terribly jealous of his original idea, which he'd quite simply stolen from me before I'd known to have it. I too would've liked to ask this of her, but it was too late now, and besides, my boss already had, in addition to this interloper, two children of her own.

* * *

THEY REAPPEARED AT ARBITRARY MOMENTS, according to their own capricious calendar, springing up by chance from one thought or another, or awaiting us at the end of a long digression; they resurfaced after a few years or remained ever present in our minds. They peopled daily life. They hovered above our heads and warned us against certain dangers, for in thinking of a tragedy or a fatal accident that had befallen someone we knew, we were forced to pay attention. Some stories would come back to us with all the catchiness of a pop song chorus, a few overheard notes enough to set it playing, and then we'd find ourselves humming it over and over all day long without choosing or wanting to. Most of the stories were somehow linked to those who'd told them, and the details surrounding their telling, too, remained bizarrely present. This was how the death of the motorcyclist who was enamored with speed—he'd worked at a café where the narrator of his crash was a regular—became strangely associated with the perfectly bland decor of the restaurant *sous-sol* where his violent end was described: with the images of a soccer match projected on the giant screen before a group of increasingly drunk Koreans, the embossed patterns on a recycled paper napkin stained with smudges of noodle broth, and the slightly forced smile of the waitress whose tight red suit and black stilettos were curiously chic for the place.

You MIGHT ON OCCASION DRAW a momentary blank, forgetting people with whom, for instance, you'd gone to school, then quite suddenly recall having learned a few weeks earlier—with no further details—that that tall fellow, one of the most memorable students at Beaux-Arts, was also dead. And all at once you'd remember the giant, stooping beanpole with his straw-colored hair hanging down to his shoulders and that long nose flanked by dark creases (in your sketchbook of classmates-as-animals, he'd been the Afghan hound), who played the clown between classes, often mimicking the peculiar laugh of one of your instructors, his deep, booming voice launching into a *TSSSSSS* that echoed throughout the studios and made you shudder and smile at once. On immense rolls of paper that he spread out and tacked to the wall, this boy made huge charcoal drawings—portraits of his mother in which she resembled a witch or a prostitute, wrinkled and decrepit, lying naked on a bed or with a small white dog in her lap. And then there was that other classmate, stocky and dark haired, with thick eyebrows, silky lashes and eyes black as obsidian, who seemed to already be seriously engaged in artistic thought. He could often be spotted in film class on Fridays, one of a group of loyal aficionados who gathered in a lecture hall where there was always some problem with cables and connections, and the professor, a former Cahiers du Cinema critic who dreamed of directing films, took half an hour to track down the remote control and make the first image appear on the tiny monitor.

At the end of the morning, everyone would join him for lunch at one of the three charmless cafes in the newly built town, and they'd draw out the discussion over a frugal croque monsieur that seemed a product of the same radical mentality they cultivated at the school, one that apparently reached as far as the brasserie's kitchen: a refusal to charm, a fear of being tricked by prettiness, and a penchant for minimalism. Then the whole group would return to the lecture hall and huddle in the dark, with stomachs tied in knots from an overly strong and bitter espresso, to watch a second or third film and discuss some more. One day, the former students learned that their dark-haired classmate with the velvety gaze had killed himself in his studio after draining a bottle of whiskey.

Not long before that, they'd found out while reading the newspaper from back to front that their old professor, who must have been lonely and deeply depressed, had also put an end to his life, that he'd made the same final gesture as a filmmaker he admired and to whom he had devoted a book.

Sometimes, after running into people you hadn't seen in ages, you might find yourself on a street corner or at a bus stop, taking a hasty inventory of all the friends you'd kept track of or who were now absent. You'd slip into a roll call of shared acquaintances, only the details you'd gathered about their lives were spotty at best, and in the end you rarely ever knew

what had happened to this person or that. Having stumbled
into the neatly coiffed bob an old school friend's mother had
sported for years—she hadn't changed much aside from her
hair which, thick as ever, was now streaked with gray—you
learned (at once touched by this reunion and unnerved by all
the things it suddenly brought to mind; a bit impatient, too,
with the slowness of her speech, which had clearly worsened
with age) that one of the twins, whose identical appearance
had so impressed everyone at school in those days, had pre-
maturely left this world.

CLASS PHOTOS TOLD MUCH THE same story: pictures of generations of schoolchildren—lined up by height, either seated or
standing, by a photographer who could gauge their dimen-
sions with a quick glance but who also, according to certain
students who resented being stuck with the little kids when
they were just as tall as the others, sometimes flubbed it—
told the story of how their paths would diverge and lead off
in unknown directions. Those smiling, glum-eyed or gri-
macing children who waited somewhat dubiously for a bird
to pop out of the camera, who posed in front of chestnut
trees and brick facades with identical windows, all those
perfectly aligned faces told you, one by one, that they would
have totally disparate and unrelated destinies; that some
would lead calm, uneventful lives, while others would suffer

terrible fates, fall seriously ill, mourn several loved ones, or, on the contrary, would find themselves blessed with luck and opportunity, would settle abroad, move to the countryside, take over the apartments and businesses of their parents in the neighborhoods where they grew up. Seeing all those eyes looking straight ahead, the contours of faces brought together for a moment by an accident of geography and the fact that they were about the same age; seeing the silhouettes of children who played together for now but would lose touch far sooner than they imagined, you could be quite certain that in just a few years it would be impossible to reassemble the exact same group. You'd wonder, too, how they might have changed in appearance or manner, which ones you would still recognize, and which would have become other people entirely.

Every so often, you'd catch yourself thinking of all the people whose lives were now far removed from yours yet whose names kept coming back to mind, always just as familiar. You never got very far, though, in the exercise of imagining what they'd done in life, whether for lack of concrete details or of the desire to seek them out, and besides, it was better not to learn too much, not to hope for a reunion, in order to spare you both the pain of having to endure those awkward attempts to fill the silence once you sat down together, or your mutual helplessness when faced with the almost inevitable, utterly depressing collapse of all complicity.

ONE DAY, AFTER OPENING THE newspaper on the terrace of a
café, your eye landed on a portrait of him at the center of
a black and white page. At first it was surprising to see a
photo of this face that had grown familiar to you after multiple sightings at the Cinémathèque without knowing the
occasion for this special recognition, and, weirdly, your
first impulse was to say his name out loud as if you wanted
to identify him before any of the other readers, or at least
before the people sitting next to you at the table, their newspapers still folded up in front of them. This momentary ela-
tion quickly gave way to a terrible shock when your gaze fell
on the headline announcing he'd died two days before. Was
he being described as a director or a filmmaker? He had himself written an essay on the question, in which he sought to
define precisely what distinguished the two: in short, the
director-cum-filmmaker had developed a body of work, a
particular universe whose existence added a new stone to
the edifice of cinema, and more often than not, it wasn't up
to them, but to history, to decide. As you flipped through
the newspaper on the café terrace before an espresso whose
thin layer of foam—for the moment, intact—hid the black-
ness beneath, your eye distracted by the dance of an amne-
siac pigeon that kept pecking at the same old cigarette butt
twenty times in a row, you experienced the discouraging
sensation that things came too quickly to an end, always cut
short at the wrong moment (but how could it be otherwise?),

while a ray of morning sun warmed the air and lines of cars waited, engines revving, at the crossroads.

AND THEN THERE WERE THOSE awful scenes glimpsed fleetingly on the side of the highway, while police in fluorescent vests waved you on so as to keep traffic moving: the mangled body-work of cars and the revolving red lights, the fleets of ambulances, or that car you spotted one night as you rounded a sharp curve in the expressway, completely flipped over, an arm sticking out from underneath. On a corner of the rue du Faubourg Saint-Antoine, in an area cordoned off by security tape, a policeman had the presence of mind to ask passersby to look away as he motioned for the trucker, who surely hadn't seen the cyclist coming from the rue de la Forge Royale—his head now crushed beneath the enormous tire—to go into reverse.

On the avenue des Pyrénées, a brown blanket was thrown over the body of a man who'd just leaped into the void. An absurdly isolated, unpaired shoe had been flung slightly farther away, and a thick ribbon of blood escaped from beneath the blanket, tracing a line on the pavement.

RETURNING HOME ONE NIGHT AFTER a brief absence, he noticed a pool of blood on the floor, and as he made his way through the rooms of the apartment, gradually discovered that his roommate had decided to end things in the most viciously painful manner at his disposal: by swallowing a bottle of drain cleaner.

WHILE THEY WERE TIDYING THE attic room where he stored some of his books, his friend, who had come along simply to chat and leaf through a few old volumes on heraldry or mycology, received a phone call and learned that his sister had jumped off the roof of her building earlier that afternoon.

THE WOMAN, WHO CONTINUED TO grow older and had only just begun to understand why, after a certain age, the vast majority of people no longer bothered celebrating their birthday, was introduced by a mutual friend to an Italian writer who lived in Rome and whom she contacted the moment she arrived there, having planned to stay in the city for a few months and wanting to go out in the evenings and meet locals. He was older than she was, a bachelor and likely a bit of an alcoholic, and had lived for years in a slightly antiquated building on a residential avenue, in an apartment his uncle had left him. This was seen as an oddity in his bohemian circle, not in keeping with his style nor with his standard of living, and they all gently mocked his absurdly privileged situation, as if he were an imposter on foreign soil.

The writer pretended to be amused by it, too, even though he actually found it a little disconcerting and had always sensed a hint of reproach in their jokes about the affluence of his neighborhood and the cachet of his apartment. The only way to make this anomaly seem acceptable to his friends who lived in neighborhoods farther from the city center or near the train station was to refer to it himself as an eccentricity. And so she called him as soon as she arrived in Rome and they saw each other many times at his apartment or in the wine bars he liked to frequent, and to this day, she wonders why he agreed so often and so kindly to take her out when it was clear that nothing would ever happen between them and both knew that this somewhat forced affiliation would last only as long as her time in the city. He was probably lonely, just as she might have been, and he must have liked the idea of this casual friendship that they nonetheless maintained by calling each other regularly. She'd even tried to film him describing a moment of guilt he'd experienced in life; they very seriously prepared for the shoot and even discussed which anecdote he might choose. Finally, seated on a folding chair in an old painter's studio, he explained to the camera that, morally, he felt quite bad about eating octopus salad since he'd heard that octopuses were among the most intelligent animals, and it bothered him to chew on a creature that might possibly be aware, sharply conscious, in fact—even once slain and boiled—of its suffering.

A few years later, she had the occasion to return to Italy
for a few days, and it seemed perfectly natural and fitting,
after so much time had passed and so many life events had no
doubt taken place, that she should surprise him with a visit.
She no longer had his phone number but needed only to type
his name into a search engine to discover a free encyclopedia
page where his life was recounted in the past tense and, scroll-
ing down a little further, she learned, two years too late, that
he'd died in a motorcycle accident.

SHE HAD, FOR SOME YEARS, been attached to several objects
that held sentimental value: for instance, a tub of coral-pink
lip gloss—a typical mother-to-daughter gift, bright and
very "springy," or so said the saleswoman at the perfum-
ery in Honfleur, and unquestionably more charming than
the greasy, overdramatic kohl that always prompted people
to ask why young women insisted on wearing all that eye
makeup—which she'd kept for years and years until it began
to resemble nothing so much as a lumpy paste, as if ravaged
by a strange affection. She'd kept a number of cards and letters as relics, while many others were lost, incomprehensibly,
though she told herself now that it was quite possible she'd
tossed them out in a moment of youthful carelessness—
letters that, in the end, contained little apart from a few
anecdotes about the other family members, primarily the cat

and the tiny dog. Those missives sent to her at summer camp or on language study trips often had to do with what these animals might feel, likely as a metaphor for feelings the writer didn't dare express directly. She found in one of them the lines: *Zoë thinks her milk is served too cold, she reproached me again for it this morning; and Tartine often curls up on your empty bed and looks up at us sadly... What a pathetic picture!*

It took years—but truly, years—for the twenty-seven-year-old woman to realize something that had never before occurred to her; that the dog's name was only one letter removed from her mother's.

In that scant pile of correspondence, there was a birthday card with a picture of a cat wearing braids and a floral dress, drawn in black, sinuous lines. Above this, a caption in the style of Magritte's paintings read *Nattes à Chat,* cat's braids. She'd always wondered if this Natacha wasn't the image of the ideal daughter her mother would have preferred, a daughter with long hair and glossy lips, well-mannered and smiling, light years from the self-conscious tomboy who always dragged her feet and sat slumped on the sofa.

A MAN WHO LIKED WEARING a fragrance made from the essence of fig leaves once wrote that the best day of his life might already be behind him. For the nearly forty-two-year-old woman, the idea of the best day was a great mystery.

That remarkable feat, a kind of chef-d'oeuvre that gracefully unfolded from morning to night and was meant to shed a light on more dismal periods to follow—did it ever really arrive? The notion of such a thing placed an enormous pressure on life itself, to be able to boast of producing a best day; and if such a day were to truly stand out from the rest, it would have to be free of any incidents, from beginning to end, with nothing to break its continuity or threaten to cast a shadow over the scene; otherwise, you'd have to swap it out for another day down the line and start all over again in the hope of, this time, achieving a flawless performance. If, for example, following a marvelous night, the day were to begin promisingly, with good news and the warmth of morning sunshine and yet, a while later, someone bumped into you on the street without apologizing, or you missed the metro by a few seconds, everything would be irrevocably ruined; a series of annoyances, even tiny ones, was enough to take that day out of the running. Even the slightest disturbance or the most trivial setback could undermine and call into question all the happy moments that had come before it.

What's more, if she'd gotten married—it's often said that your wedding is supposed to be the happiest day of your life— she'd surely have spent every minute of her day on the lookout for blunders, obsessing over the smallest detail or gaffe, from a guest's yawn or the alcohol on a waiter's breath to the toughness of the meat, when they'd certainly ordered prime quality.

She'd be determined to uncover any scrap of evidence that could contradict this cliché, as if seeking to distance herself, despite all she felt for her future husband, from the notion that marriage represents the pinnacle of happiness in a woman's life. Something contrarian and a bit superstitious in her would be determined to prove that these grandiose sayings, so often drummed into us, also have their margin of error and don't always apply to the whole of humanity.

Besides, people spoke more often of the best day than of the worst day. You almost never wondered what your most sinister day would look like or when it would take place. No one—it was just as well—thought *hmm, what do you make of this one: might it not be the worst day of your life?*

WE'D GET READY TO LEAVE the little square after sitting there for a long while, gazing at the serrated leaves and the arcs of water that splashed onto the sand whenever a child reached up to press the fountain button with both hands. She would no doubt want to return to the kingdom of souls, having understood that she wouldn't really be able to adapt to life here below. I'd try to change her mind, but would soon run out of persuasive arguments. Then I'd hear myself proclaiming *c'est beau la vie*, but it would just make me think of a slogan for gummy candies, and I'd watch as she disappeared again, trudging up the avenue to have one more look at the crocodile leather sofas and other tawdry pieces of furniture in the shop windows before rounding a corner to the right and taking the long street that leads up to Père-Lachaise.

As I turned and started in the opposite direction, I'd wonder what had happened to the lady who sold flowers at the market and whose magnificent dahlias, apparently grown in her tiny suburban garden, she wrapped in newspaper and tied with a wisp of wool, blaming mother nature for the fact that she didn't have them every week, though she offered in their place no less fabulous bouquets of snapdragons and bluebonnets. And the tiny, wrinkled woman who waited on the doorstep of her stationary shop, fists plunged into the kangaroo pocket of her polyester blouse, making the fabric sag even though her hands couldn't have weighed very much at all, and who always looked out at the street from that same position, filled with the undying hope that a few schoolchildren might come in to buy the stickers and slightly faded notebooks on display in the little window case.

A FEW YARDS FARTHER ON, the street would be packed as usual with people crossing paths and weaving around each other, meandering along or hurrying off to appointments, pedaling on bicycles so as not to be late. It would be teeming with passersby continually moving forward, trying to stay on course, to avoid a puddle, to catch someone's eye, while above their heads, in an apartment situated several stories high, a man might have stopped wondering what he would do the next day. Arms would lift boxes, carry bags, swing to the rhythm of footsteps; legs would turn in one direction or the other, march straight ahead, take the stairs. Minds would consider a thousand things, would pursue the thread of an idea, would recall an old phrase or two, dreaming relentlessly of some paradise.

TRANSLATOR'S NOTE

If we storytellers are Death's Secretaries,
we are so because, in our brief mortal lives,
we are grinders of these lenses.
—John Berger, *And Our Faces, My Heart, Brief as Photos*

G IVEN THE CHOICE, WOULD YOU rather know when—the precise moment—you were going to die, or how? A friend asked me this pithy question a few months ago, when I was in the final stages of editing the translation you've just read. I thought about it for a moment, then said it wouldn't make all that much difference to me, so long as Valérie Mréjen wrote my obituary. How to explain to my friend: the lightness of hand, the quiet intensity of attention, the knack for finding poignancy in the banally absurd, all so distinctively Mréjen's? Who wouldn't want the postscript to their life to be handled with such care?

Of course, Mréjen's approach to writing about death—its sly, callous inventiveness and the transformations wrought by it on the living—is formally more akin to the witness statement than to the obituary. Her aim is not to eulogize but to detail, to inventory, to record; to fulfill the role, in Berger's sense, of Death's secretary. And yet that word, *care*, is among the first that come to mind whenever I try to describe the peculiar intimacy of this writing that never once reaches for pathos. Mréjen's insistence on maintaining a certain distance from her subject feels to me rooted in care, which is to say the opposite of carelessness: vigilance, discretion, accuracy. It's as if she knew that to come any closer would be to breach some mysterious contract made with Death itself: I'll show you my face, as long as you stay right there—no sudden movements—and as long as you don't look away.

And she doesn't; not for a beat. She doesn't flinch, either. The steady focus of her gaze keeps our attention on the space of the encounter with death; an encounter that, in these pages, almost always comes as the rudest of shocks. Like the anonymous writers of *faits divers*—the brief, sordid news items used as "filler" in French newspapers of old—Mréjen catalogues the kind of sudden, tragic, odd and unexplained deaths that we secretly believe only happen to other people. She treats each one as a complete story with its own internal logic and timing, and these self-contained narratives are often devastating in their concision. But as they accumulate over the course of the novel, intertwining with the dark tale of mother and daughter that stands at its heart, the sense of a larger pattern begins to emerge: the one death's traces have left, indelibly, on a forty-something consciousness; the contours of a forest populated by ghosts.

VALÉRIE MRÉJEN WAS BORN IN 1969 in Paris and grew up in the 17th arrondissement, a leafy, quiet enclave in the northwest corner of the city. Her circuitous path to literature began at the École Nationale Supérieure d'Arts in Cergy-Pontoise, where she developed a practice in video and mixed-media arts. The videos she made after graduating—brief sketches that mine the minutiae of everyday interactions, often revolving around a failure to communicate—were widely exhibited and remain touchstones of her oeuvre. (It bears pointing out that her first video, *Une noix*, contains the seed of what would become a leitmotif in this novel and in much of her work: the way language operates within the family, especially between parents and children. In it, a young girl grows increasingly frustrated as she tries to recite a poem and is interrupted again and again by her sermonizing mother.)

Around the same time, she began working on a series of cut-up texts that mimic the language in personals ads, using only proper names found in the phonebook; the fastidious and somewhat obsessive process involved in making the cut-ups was, Mréjen later said in an interview, "an indirect way of coming to writing." Her first novel, *Mon grand-père*, published in 1999, and the two that followed in short order—*L'Agrume* (2001) and *Eau Sauvage* (2004)—are each in their own way collage-like, fragmentary texts that toy with conventions of self-portraiture. To my mind, they can be read as a sort of triptych that engages with the question of how others' words shape us, in particular when we are young and still stuttering ourselves into being. *Forêt noire* shares in those concerns to a certain extent, but if the earlier work was preoccupied with the limiting forces of language, here Mréjen acknowledges those limitations and attempts the impossible anyway: to speak at length, exclusively, and without interruption of the very thing that embodies the unsayable (for, as the saying goes, no one has come back to tell us about it).

Little surprise, then, that the novel marks a stylistic and tonal break: from the short, declarative sentences that achieve a disquieting cumulative effect in the "tryptich," to the meandering ones in *Forêt noire* that unfold like paper flowers; from the imposed flatness of tone that became Mréjen's signature early on in her career, to the seamless shifts in tense, register and point of view that run through this novel, yielding more oddity and ambiguity. My greatest challenge in translating *Forêt noire* was, without question, finding the right way to carry that strangeness over into English, and striking the delicate balance between vagueness and precision—and, by extension, between formal distance and emotional immediacy—that gives this writing its subtle dissonance.

The deeper I delved into Mrejen's sentences, the more compelled I felt to immerse myself in her particular universe, too. Whenever I hadn't been translating for a while and needed to ease into the mood of the book again, it was a comfort to spend time with the films—and the hallowed HBO series—that are woven into the narrative, each reflecting its overall tone in some way. I watched and re-watched Raymond Depardon's 1983 documentary *Faits divers*, which follows a group of cops on their daily rounds in a Paris precinct, and Ernst Lubitsch's fleet, enchanting 1943 comedy *Heaven Can Wait*, in which the boundary between the living and the dead becomes magically porous. The translating flowed more easily once I came to understand that the two films serve as counterpoints in the novel, playfully echoing its title's double meaning.[1] I revisited *Six Feet Under*, which Mréjen has said served as inspiration (and more than once, as I settled in on the couch and let the opening credits roll, I found myself gauging the distance to the bathroom door). Perhaps most significantly, I discovered a whole body of work that isn't named in the text, but that casts a shadow over it from the first sentence; that of a man who liked wearing a fragrance made from the essence of fig leaves, and who decided one day that he'd lived long enough.

---

1. Black Forest, of course, refers to both the mountain range in Germany often associated with the macabre fairy tales of the Brothers Grimm, and the decadent dessert that gets its name from that region.

Mréjen's late friend and sometimes collaborator, Édouard Levé, left behind several books of photographs and four slim volumes of deeply thoughtful, witty, enigmatic prose; in his final novel, *Suicide*, Levé's narrator addresses a friend who killed himself fifteen years earlier, at twenty-five, on his birthday, the 25th of December.[2] Mréjen's novel, too, is filled with eerie symmetries, and reading Levé's works alongside it gave me a heightened awareness of these patterns and resonances.

I first read *Forêt noire* in the winter of 2013, shortly after my grandfather died. Though it was, as they say, an easy death, it had levelled me, and I found myself unable to sleep at night, alert with the knowledge that everyone dear to me would sooner or later be taken away. During that time, this book was not only an unlikely source of consolation; reading it felt like an indulgence, too. Whenever I attempted to talk about it with someone else, I could not find words to explain the rush of pleasure—a physical buzz not unlike the one you might get from a slice or three of the titular cake—that I felt each time I picked it up again. This translation project began with that buzzy feeling, and with a desire to tease it out and understand it; at the time, I had no contract and no full-length literary translation to my name. Mréjen's graciousness and enthusi-

---

2. The author famously ended his own life ten days after delivering the manuscript to his editor at Éditions P.O.L., the same publishing house that would later add *Forêt noire* to its inimitable list.

asm kept me at it, as did a growing conviction that, while the
novel isn't for everyone—certainly not for members of the
cult of the carefree—it would find its Anglophone readers. I
hope that it comforts and unsettles them in ways they don't
yet know they need, and that it works on them in ways they're
unable to explain.

One of the interesting things about translating this book
very sporadically over a number of years was that all my drafts
and notes—all the emails and texts exchanged with Valérie,
who also became a friend—began to mark the passage of
time. With each year that's gone by (and how fitting that the
novel's opening scene should take place on New Year's Eve),
our respective forests, Valérie's and mine, have grown denser
with ghosts. On January 2nd of last year, Paul Otchakovsky-
Laurens, the beloved founder of Éditions P.O.L., died in a car
accident while on holiday with his wife in Guadeloupe. Just a
few weeks earlier, Valérie had accompanied him to a screen-
ing of his second film, *Éditeur*, which traces his decades-long
journey in publishing and investigates his relationship to his
authors. In the days that followed his death, she wrote an
essay about the film and her memories of Paul from that night.
These lines have stayed with me: *A woman takes the micro-
phone: now that you've made this film, and after so many years
in the same profession, do you think you'll go into a new line of
work or will you keep at this one until the end? (...) He shakes his
head—cheekbones lifting in a smile, neck tucked slightly between*

his shoulders—and says: you know, I've been doing this work for fifty years; if I was going to get tired of it, I already would have a long time ago. My model is Maurice Nadeau, who died still working at a hundred and two, so... (...).[3] In the space of an ellipsis, fate takes a different turn.

I WOULD LIKE TO EXPRESS my thanks to E.C. Belli, Ruggero Bozotti, Eleanor Kriseman, Chad Post, and most especially Julia Sanches for their invaluable insights over the course of the translation process. Thanks also to the editors of Joyland Magazine for publishing an early excerpt; to Veronica Esposito for helping me to find an interested publisher in Phoneme Books, and to my husband, Christian Estevez, for his cheerful support and always perceptive comments on the French. I'm indebted to the Collège Internationale des Traducteurs Littéraires in Arles for giving me time to complete final edits in a place so lovely I didn't want to leave (and haven't). Above all: thank you, Valérie Mréjen, for your patience, your unfailing kindness, and your words.

3. Mréjen, Valérie. "Au cinéma avec Paul Otchakovsky-Laurens." *Trafic* no. 105 (2018) : 7–12. Print.

VALÉRIE MRÉJEN (B. 1969) is a writer, filmmaker, and mixed-media artist. She has written five novels, most recently *Troisième personne* (P.O.L., 2017), and exhibited widely in France and abroad, including in a solo retrospective at the Jeu de Paume gallery in Paris. Mréjen has made several short films, documentaries (*Pork and Milk*, 2004; *Valvert*, 2008), and a feature-length film, *En ville*, co-directed with Bertrand Schefer and a Director's Fortnight selection at the Cannes Film Festival in 2011. She has written two original plays (*Trois hommes verts* and *Le carnaval des animaux*, a collaboration with singer-songwriter Albin de la Simone based on Camille Saint-Saëns's musical suite), and her adaptation of Alexandre Dumas *fils's La dame aux Camélias* was performed in Arthur Nauzyciel's production on stages throughout France. An alumna of residencies at Villa Medici in Rome and Villa Kujoyama in Kyoto, she is curating a 2019 exhibition based on the archives at the Institute for Contemporary Publishing (IMEC) in Normandy and working on a documentary about students at the Ecole des Beaux-Arts in Paris. More information can be found online at www.valeriemrejen.com.

KATIE SHIREEN ASSEF is a literary translator living between Los Angeles and Arles, France. *Black Forest* is her first full-length translation.

Donors & Partners

First Edition Membership

Anonymous (8)

Translator's Circle

Ben & Sharon Fountain

Meriwether Evans

Printer's Press Membership

Allred Capital Management
Robert Appel
Charles Dee Mitchell
Cullen Schaar
David Tomlinson & Kathryn Berry
Jeff Leuschel
Judy Pollock
Loretta Siciliano

Lori Feathers
Mary Ann Thompson-Frenk
& Joshua Frenk
Matthew Rittmayer
Nick Storch
Pixel and Texel
Social Venture Partners Dallas
Stephen Bullock

Author's League

Christie Tull
Farley Houston
Jacob Seifring
Lissa Dunlay

Stephen Bullock
Steven Kornajcik
Thomas DiPiero

Publisher's League

Adam Rekerdres
Christie Tull
Justin Childress

Kay Cattarulla
KMGMT
Olga Kislova

Editor's League

Amrit Dhir
Brandon Kennedy
Garth Hallberg
Greg McConeghy
Linda Nell Evans
Mike Kaminsky
Patricia Storace

Ryan Todd
Steven Harding
Suejean Kim
Symphonic Source
Wendy Belcher

THANK YOU ALL FOR YOUR SUPPORT.
WE DO THIS FOR YOU,
AND COULD NOT DO IT WITHOUT YOU.

READER'S LEAGUE

Caitlin Baker
Caroline Casey
Carolyn Mulligan
Chilton Thomson
Cody Cosmic & Jeremy Hays
Jeff Waxman
Kayla Finstein
Kelly Britson

Kelly & Corby Baxter
Marian Schwartz & Reid Minot
Marlo D. Cruz Pagan
Mary Grimaldi
Maryam Baig
Peggy Carr
Susan Ernst

ADDITIONAL DONORS

Alan Shockley
Andrew Yorke
Anonymous (9)
Anthony Messenger
Bob & Katherine Penn
Brandon Childress
Charley Mitcherson
Charley Rejsek
Cheryl Thompson
Cone Johnson
CS Maynard
Daniel J. Hale
Dori Boone-Costantino
Ed Nawotka
Elizabeth Gillette
Erin Kubatzky
Ester & Matt Harrison
Grace Kenney
JJ Italiano
Joseph Milazzo
Kelly Falconer
Laura Thomson
Lea Courington

Leigh Ann Pike
Lowell Frye
Maaza Mengiste
Mark Haber
Mary Cline
Maynard Thomson
Michael Reklis
Mike Soto
Mokhtar Ramadan
Nikki & Dennis Gibson
Patrick Kukucka
Patrick Kutcher
Rev. Elizabeth & Neil Moseley
Richard Meyer
Scott & Katy Nimmons
Sherry Perry
Stephen Harding
Susan Carp
Susan Ernst
Theater Jones
Tim Perttula
Tony Thomson